"Dream big because dreams do come true!"

I am grateful to God for his many blessings that allow me
to live my dream. A special thanks to my family, friends,
and mentors. Neither this book, nor my many other
successes would have been possible without your support.

- Earl Cooper

Earl A. Cooper
First Tee Alumni

N H.

www.mascotbooks.com

For more information, please contact:
Mascot Books
560 Herndon Parkway #120
Herndon, VA 20170
info@mascotbooks.com

CPSIA Code: PRT1213A
ISBN-10: 1620861283
ISBN-13: 9781620861288

Printed in the United States

Baby Bison's First Homecoming

BISON

HOWARD UNIVERSITY ™

Earl Anthony Cooper

Illustrated by Zantoine Truluck

It was a beautiful fall day in Washington, DC for the Howard University Homecoming. His parents had explained what would happen at the Homecoming. There would be a weekend celebration attended by people of all ages. Many of the people would be alumni who were past students who had attended and graduated from Howard. The city was filled with students and alumni ready to have lots of fun at homecoming. This homecoming was extra special because it was Baby Bison's first one!

Baby Bison's parents, Big Blue and Lady Blue, had an important job to do. Not only were they the mascots for Howard University, but they also needed to give their son a campus tour.

As they started their journey through the Tubman Quadrangle, a freshman area also known as "The Quad," Lady Blue explained to Baby Bison, "This building was named after Harriet Tubman. She was leader of the Underground Railroad."

As their journey continued through campus, they stopped in front of Rankin Chapel. They saw a group of students gathered out front.

One of the students stopped the Bison family and asked, "Is this Baby Bison's first visit to Howard?"

His mother told them, "Yes!"

The students said, "Welcome, Baby Bison!"

Baby Bison waved shyly, "Hi."

Another one of the students asked him, "Would you like to learn a song, Baby Bison?"

He eagerly nodded his head yes.

The students began singing a beautiful song. He loved the music and how happy the students looked while they were singing it! Baby Bison asked how all the students knew the words to the song. His father explained that schools often have an official song that all the students learn that is called the school's alma mater. Then Baby Bison understood. They were singing their school's song!
Baby Bison wanted them to sing it again but his father said it was time to say goodbye. There was more to see and they couldn't be late for the football game!

Next, the Bison family walked to The Yard. Many historical buildings surround The Yard. They were named after important leaders throughout history. Baby Bison could see C.B. Powell Hall, Alain Locke Hall, and Lulu Vere Childers Hall, just to name a few.

Baby Bison saw many Howard alumni enjoying friends on The Yard. He also noticed students wearing matching colors. They were fraternity and sorority members practicing their steps for a friendly stroll-off after the game.

"We're glad you are here, Baby Bison," they told him. They asked if they could take a picture with him and his parents.

When they were walking away, Big Blue looked down at the smiling Baby Bison and said, "You know, son, Howard University is the place where most African American fraternities and sororities began."

The Bison family passed by Cramton Auditorium. Students, alumni, and fans were getting some last minute tickets for the homecoming football game. "We don't need a ticket," Big Blue told Baby Bison. "We'll be down on the field!"

Everyone was very excited about the game. Baby Bison smiled brightly as he waved to news reporters that drove by in the WHUR Radio and TV van. They were going to the stadium to broadcast the game. "Wow!" exclaimed Baby Bison. "Howard University has its own radio and television station. I would like to work there one day."

Inside Greene Memorial Stadium, Baby Bison couldn't believe his eyes. There were so many people excited about the game. He clapped as his mother and father helped the Howard cheerleaders lead the crowd in singing the Howard Fight Song.

"Touchdown Bisons!" the announcer called out, and the crowd cheered loudly. After the first half, it was a close game. Howard was ahead of their rival by only three points.

The Showtime Marching Band went onto the field. The drum major had the marching band sounding great! The crowd was following every move. Band members put on a great halftime performance.

It was almost time for the second half of the game to begin. Baby Bison and his dad got in the huddle with the team before they ran back onto the field. They all put their hands together in the air and yelled, "Let's go, HU!" Baby bison was so excited! He ran out the huddle and led the Howard football team back onto the field.

The last minute of the game had everyone sitting on the edge of their seats. When Howard completed another touchdown, the crowd began chanting, "HU, you know!"

The Bisons won! Baby Bison was having a wonderful time at his first Howard University football game.

After such an exciting game, everyone was hungry. The Bison family went to Punchout to enjoy a victory meal with other fans. When they got there, everyone was talking about the win.

As his family left campus, Baby Bison was tired from a day of fun but all he could think about was coming back to Howard Homecoming next year! Like his mother and father, he wanted to be a Howard Bison, too!

Once they arrived home, Baby Bison got ready for bed. He told his mom and dad, "Thank you for a great day. I am going to keep doing my best in school so I can be a Howard University student."

His parents gave him a hug and said, "You're welcome, son. Goodnight."

A Little History

General Oliver Otis Howard founded Howard University, a historically black university in 1867 in Washington, DC, to train African American preachers, teachers, and doctors after the Civil War. Over 10,000 students from around the world study there each year. Howard produces more on-campus African American Ph.D.s than any other university in the world. The school's motto is Veritas et Utilitas – Truth and Service. Learn more about Howard University at www.howard.edu.

QUESTIONS TO INTRODUCE THE COLLEGE EXPERIENCE AT HOWARD UNIVERSITY

Do you want to go to college? Why?

Does Baby Bison seem to be having fun? Why?

How many places did Baby Bison visit? Which was your favorite?

Can you imagine yourself as a student at Howard University?

What would be your major or favorite subject?

Would you join the marching band, a sorority, a fraternity, play sports, or work at the Howard radio and television station?

CHECK THE THINGS YOU CAN DO SO YOU WILL BE PREPARED TO GO TO COLLEGE:

- [ ] Do your best in school.
- [ ] Do chores at home to learn responsibility.
- [ ] Help others in your community.

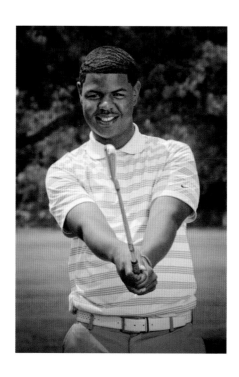

ABOUT THE AUTHOR

Earl Anthony Cooper graduated from Morehouse College in 2011 with a B.A. in political science. He was instrumental in leading his alma mater to its first National Golf Championship in 2010. Prior to attending Morehouse, Earl was an all-state golfer for the state of Delaware and has continued to earn many golf honors and achievements. He completed the PGA (Professional Golf Association) Post-Graduate Program and is pursuing a professional golf career. Earl Anthony knew little about Historically Black Colleges and Universities (HBCUs) growing up. He is happy *Baby Bison's First Homecoming* and his first book, *Hello, Maroon Tiger!* about Morehouse college are introducing children to the HBCU legacy. His challenge as he travels and speaks to young people is to "Dream B.I.G. (Because I'm Great) because dreams do come true!" Contact him at www.earldreambig.com.

www.earldreambig.com

ABOUT THE ARTIST

Zantoine (Zan) Truluck began his career as an illustrator after graduating from Morehouse College in 2009. A native of Baltimore, Maryland by way of Brooklyn, New York, Zan received fine arts training for seven years prior to college– during which time he gained a passion for charcoal drawing, sculpting, and oil painting.

Zan approaches his illustrations as if they are an oil painting and makes sure to include some level of realism in each illustration no matter how far-reaching the subject matter, leaving all his work with a style that is uniquely his own. From drawing his favorite Ninja Turtles as a child to now illustrating some children's new favorite characters, Zan truly enjoys making his passion his work.